he telling or reading of ghost stories during long, dark and cold Christmas nights is a yuletide ritual which dates to at least the eighteenth century, and was once as much a part of Christmas tradition as decorating fir trees, feasting on goose and the singing of carols. During the Victorian era many magazines printed ghost stories specifically for the Christmas season. These "winter tales" did not necessarily explore Christmas themes in any manner. Rather, they were offered as an eerie pleasure to be enjoyed on Christmas eve with the family, adding a supernatural shiver to the seasonal chill.

This tradition remained strong in the British Isles (and her colonies) throughout much of the twentieth century, though in recent years it has been on the wane. Certainly, few people in Canada or the United States seem to know about it any longer. This series of small books seeks to rectify this, to revive a charming custom for the long, dark nights we all know so well here at Christmastime.

THE CROWN DERBY PLATE

The CROWN DERBY PLATE

MARJORIE BOWEN

A GHOST STORY FOR CHRISTMAS
DESIGNED & DECORATED BY SETH

BIBLIOASIS

artha Pym said that she had never seen a ghost and that she would very much like to do so, "particularly at Christmas, for you can laugh as you like, that is the correct time to see a ghost."

"I don't suppose you ever will," replied her cousin Mabel comfortably, while her cousin Clara shuddered and said that she hoped they would change the subject for she disliked even to think of such things.

The three elderly, cheerful women sat round a big fire, cosy and content after a day of pleasant activities; Martha was the guest of the other two, who owned the handsome, convenient country house; she always came to spend her Christmas with the Wyntons and found the leisurely country life delightful after the bustling round of London, for Martha managed an antique shop of the better sort and worked extremely hard. She was, however, still full of zest for work or pleasure, though sixty years old, and looked backwards and forwards to a succession of delightful days.

The other two, Mabel and Clara, led quieter but none the less agreeable lives; they had more money and fewer interests, but nevertheless enjoyed themselves very well.

"Talking of ghosts," said Mabel, "I wonder how that old woman at 'Hartleys' is getting on, for 'Hartleys,' you know, is supposed to be haunted."

"Yes, I know," smiled Miss Pym, "but all the years that we have known of the place we have never heard anything definite, have we?"

"No," put in Clara; "but there is that persistent rumour that the House is uncanny, and for myself, nothing would induce me to live there!"

"It is certainly very lonely and dreary down there on the marshes," conceded Mabel. "But as for the ghost—you never hear what it is supposed to be even."

"Who has taken it?" asked Miss Pym, remembering "Hartleys" as very desolate indeed, and long shut up.

"A Miss Lefain, an eccentric old creature—I think you met her here once, two years ago—"

"I believe that I did, but I don't recall her at all."

"We have not seen her since, 'Hartleys' is so un-get-at-able and she didn't seem to want visitors. She collects china, Martha, so really you ought to go and see her and talk 'shop.'"

With the word "china" some curious associations came into the mind of Martha Pym; she was silent while she strove to put them together, and after a second or two they all fitted together into a very clear picture.

She remembered that thirty years ago—yes, it must be thirty years ago, when, as a young woman, she had put all her capital into the antique business, and had been staying with her cousins (her aunt had then been alive) that she had driven across the marsh to "Hartleys," where there was an auction sale; all the details of this she had completely forgotten, but she could recall quite clearly purchasing a set of gorgeous china which was still one of her proud delights, a perfect set of Crown Derby save that one plate was missing.

"How odd," she remarked, "that this Miss Lefain should collect china too, for it was at 'Hartleys' that I purchased my dear old Derby service—I've never been able to match that plate—"

"A plate was missing? I seem to remember," said Clara. "Didn't they say that it must be in the house somewhere and that it should be looked for?"

"I believe they did, but of course I never heard any more and that missing plate has annoyed me ever since. Who had 'Hartleys'?"

"An old connoisseur, Sir James Sewell; I believe he was some relation to this Miss Lefain, but I don't know—"

"I wonder if she has found the plate," mused Miss Pym. "I expect she has turned out and ransacked the whole place—"

"Why not trot over and ask?" suggested Mabel. "It's not much use to her, if she has found it, one odd plate."

"Don't be silly," said Clara. "Fancy going over the marshes, this weather, to ask about a plate missed all those years ago. I'm sure Martha wouldn't think of it—"

But Martha did think of it; she was rather fascinated by the idea; how queer and pleasant it would be if, after all these years, nearly a lifetime, she should find the Crown Derby plate, the loss of which had always irked her! And this hope did not seem so altogether fantastical, it was quite likely that old Miss Lefain, poking about in the ancient house, had found the missing piece.

And, of course, if she had, being a fellow-collector, she would be quite willing to part with it to complete the set.

Her cousin endeavoured to dissuade her; Miss Lefain, she declared, was a recluse, an odd creature who might greatly resent such a visit and such a request.

"Well, if she does I can but come away again," smiled Miss Pym. "I suppose she can't bite my head off, and I rather like meeting these curious types—we've got a love for old china in common, anyhow."

"It seems so silly to think of it—after all these years—a plate!"

"A Crown Derby plate," corrected Miss Pym. "It is certainly strange that I didn't think of it before, but now that I have got it into my head I can't get it out. Besides," she added hopefully, "I might see the ghost."

So full, however, were the days with pleasant local engagements that Miss Pym had no immediate chance of putting her scheme into practice; but she did not relinquish it, and she asked several different people what they knew about "Hartleys" and Miss Lefain.

And no one knew anything save that the house was supposed to be haunted and the owner "cracky."

"Is there a story?" asked Miss Pym, who associated ghosts with neat tales into which they fitted as exactly as nuts into shells.

But she was always told: "Oh, no, there isn't a story, no one knows anything about the place, don't know how the idea got about; old Sewell was half-crazy, I believe, he was buried in the garden and that gives a house a nasty name"

"Very unpleasant," said Martha Pym, undisturbed.

This ghost seemed too elusive for her to track down; she would have to be content if she could recover the Crown Derby plate; for that at least she was determined to make a try and also to satisfy that faint tingling of curiosity roused in her by this talk about "Hartleys" and the remembrance of that day, so long ago, when she had gone to the auction sale at the lonely old house.

So the first free afternoon, while Mabel and Clara were comfortably taking their afternoon repose, Martha Pym, who was of a more lively habit, got out her little governess cart and dashed away across the Essex flats.

She had taken minute directions with her, but she had soon lost her way.

Under the wintry sky, which looked as grey and hard as metal, the marshes stretched bleakly to the horizon, the olive-brown broken reeds were harsh as scars on the saffron-tinted bogs, where the sluggish waters that rose so high in winter were filmed over with the first stillness of a frost; the air was cold but not keen, everything was damp; faintest of mists blurred the black outlines of trees that rose stark from the ridges above the stagnant dykes; the flooded fields were haunted by black birds and white birds, gulls and crows, whining above the long ditch grass and wintry wastes.

Miss Pym stopped the little horse and surveyed this spectral scene, which had a certain relish about it to one sure to return to a homely village, a cheerful house and good company.

A withered and bleached old man, in colour like the dun landscape, came along the road between the sparse alders.

Miss Pym, buttoning up her coat, asked the way to "Hartley" as he passed her; he told her, straight on, and she proceeded, straight indeed across the road that went with undeviating length across the marshes.

"Of course," thought Miss Pym, "if you live in a place like this, you are bound to invent ghosts."

The house sprang up suddenly on a knoll ringed with rotting trees, encompassed by an old brick wall that the perpetual damp had overrun with lichen, blue, green, white colours of decay.

"Hartleys," no doubt, there was no other residence of human being in sight in all the wide expanse; besides, she could remember it, surely, after all this time, the sharp rising out of the marsh, the colony of tall trees, but then fields and trees had been green and bright—there had been no water on the flats, it had been summer-time.

"She certainly," thought Miss Pym, "must be crazy to live here. And I rather doubt if I shall get my plate."

She fastened up the good little horse by the garden gate which stood negligently ajar and entered; the garden itself was so neglected that it was quite surprising to see a trim appearance in the house, curtains at the window and a polish on the brass door knocker, which must have been recently rubbed there, considering the taint in the sea damp which rusted and rotted everything.

It was a square-built, substantial house with "nothing wrong with it but the situation," Miss Pym decided, though it was not very attractive, being built of that drab plastered stone so popular a hundred years ago, with flat windows and door, while one side was gloomily shaded by a large evergreen tree of the cypress variety which gave a blackish tinge to that portion of the garden.

There was no pretence at flower-beds nor any manner of cultivation in this garden where a few rank weeds and straggling bushes matted together above the dead grass; on the enclosing wall which appeared to have been built high as protection against the ceaseless winds that swung along the flats were the remains of fruit trees; their crucified branches, rotting under the great nails that held them up, looked like the skeletons of those who had died in torment.

Miss Pym took in these noxious details as she knocked firmly at the door; they did not depress her; she merely felt extremely sorry for anyone who could live in such a place.

She noticed, at the far end of the garden, in the corner of the wall, a headstone showing above the sodden colourless grass, and remembered what she had been told about the old antiquary being buried there, in the grounds of "Hartleys."

As the knock had no effect she stepped back and looked at the house; it was certainly inhabited—with those neat windows, white curtains and drab blinds all pulled to precisely the same level.

And when she brought her glance back to the door she saw that it had been opened and that someone, considerably obscured by the darkness of the passage, was looking at her intently.

"Good afternoon," said Miss Pym cheerfully. "I just thought that I would call to see Miss Lefain—it is Miss Lefain, isn't it?"

"It's my house," was the querulous reply.

Martha Pym had hardly expected to find any servants here, though the old lady must, she thought, work pretty hard to keep the house so clean and tidy as it appeared to be.

"Of course," she replied. "May I come in? I'm Martha Pym, staying with the Wyntons, I met you there"

"Do come in," was the faint reply. "I get so few people to visit me, I'm really very lonely."

"I don't wonder," thought Miss Pym; but she had resolved to take no notice of any eccentricity on the part of her hostess, and so she entered the house with her usual agreeable candour and courtesy.

The passage was badly lit, but she was able to get a fair idea of Miss Lefain; her first impression was that this poor creature was most dreadfully old, older than any human being had the right to be, why, she felt young in comparison—so faded, feeble, and pallid was Miss Lefain.

She was also monstrously fat; her gross, flaccid figure was shapeless and she wore a badly cut, full dress of no colour at all, but stained with earth and damp where Miss Pym supposed she had been doing futile gardening; this gown was doubtless designed to disguise her stoutness, but had been so carelessly pulled about that it only added to it, being rucked and rolled "all over the place" as Miss Pym put it to herself.

Another ridiculous touch about the appearance of the poor old lady was her short hair; decrepit as she was, and lonely as she lived she had actually had her scanty relics of white hair cropped round her shaking head.

"Dear me, dear me," she said in her thin treble voice. "How very kind of you to come. I suppose you prefer the parlour? I generally sit in the garden."

"The garden? But not in this weather?"

"I get used to the weather. You've no idea how used one gets to the weather."

"I suppose so," conceded Miss Pym doubtfully. "You don't live here quite alone, do you?"

"Quite alone, lately. I had a little company, but she was taken away, I'm sure I don't know where. I haven't been able to find a trace of her anywhere," replied the old lady peevishly.

"Some wretched companion that couldn't stick it, I suppose," thought Miss Pym. "Well, I don't wonder—but someone ought to be here to look after her."

They went into the parlour, which, the visitor was dismayed to see, was without a fire but otherwise well kept.

And there, on dozens of shelves was a choice array of china at which Martha Pym's eyes glistened.

"Aha!" cried Miss Lefain. "I see you've noticed my treasures! Don't you envy me? Don't you wish that you had some of those pieces?"

Martha Pym certainly did and she looked eagerly and greedily round the walls, tables, and cabinets while the old woman followed her with little thin squeals of pleasure.

It was a beautiful little collection, most choicely and elegantly arranged, and Martha thought it marvellous that this feeble ancient creature should be able to keep it in such precise order as well as doing her own housework.

"Do you really do everything yourself here and live quite alone?" she asked, and she shivered even in her thick coat and wished that Miss Lefain's energy had risen to a fire, but then probably she lived in the kitchen, as these lonely eccentrics often did.

"There was someone," answered Miss Lefain cunningly, "but I had to send her away. I told you she's gone, I can't find her, and I am so glad. Of course," she added wistfully, "it leaves me very lonely, but then I couldn't stand her impertinence any longer. She used to say that it was her house and her collection of china! Would you believe it? She used to try to chase me away from looking at my own things!"

"How very disagreeable," said Miss Pym, wondering which of the two women had been crazy. "But hadn't you better get someone else."

"Oh, no," was the jealous answer. "I would rather be alone with my things, I daren't leave the house for fear someone takes them away—there was a dreadful time once when an auction sale was held here"

"Were you here then?" asked Miss Pym; but indeed she looked old enough to have been anywhere.

"Yes, of course," Miss Lefain replied rather peevishly and Miss Pym decided that she must be a relation of old Sir James

Sewell. Clara and Mabel had been very foggy about it all. "I was very busy hiding all the china—but one set they got—a Crown Derby tea service"

"With one plate missing!" cried Martha Pym. "I bought it, and do you know, I was wondering if you'd found it"

"I hid it," piped Miss Lefain.

"Oh, you did, did you? Well, that's rather funny behaviour. Why did you hide the stuff away instead of buying it?"

"How could I buy what was mine?"

"Old Sir James left it to you, then?" asked Martha Pym, feeling very muddled.

"She bought a lot more," squeaked Miss Lefain, but Martha Pym tried to keep her to the point.

"If you've got the plate," she insisted, "you might let me have it—I'll pay quite handsomely, it would be so pleasant to have it after all these years."

"Money is no use to me," said Miss Lefain mournfully. "Not a bit of use. I can't leave the house or the garden."

"Well, you have to live, I suppose," replied Martha Pym cheerfully. "And, do you know, I'm afraid you are getting rather morbid and dull, living here all alone—you really ought to have a fire—why, it's just on Christmas and very damp."

"I haven't felt the cold for a long time," replied the other; she seated herself with a sigh on one of the horsehair chairs and Miss Pym noticed with a start that her feet were covered only by a pair of white stockings; "one of those nasty health fiends," thought Miss Pym, "but she doesn't look too well for all that."

"So you don't think that you could let me have the plate?" she asked briskly, walking up and down, for the dark, neat, clean parlour was very cold indeed, and she thought that she couldn't stand this much longer; as there seemed no sign of tea or anything pleasant and comfortable she had really better go.

"I might let you have it," sighed Miss Lefain, "since you've been so kind as to pay me a visit. After all, one plate isn't much use, is it?"

"Of course not, I wonder you troubled to hide it."

"I couldn't bear," wailed the other, "to see the things going out of the house!"

Martha Pym couldn't stop to go into all this; it was quite clear that the old lady was very eccentric indeed and that nothing very much could be done with her; no wonder that she had "dropped out" of everything and that no one ever saw her or knew anything about her, though Miss Pym felt that some effort ought really to be made to save her from herself.

"Wouldn't you like a run in my little governess cart?" she suggested. "We might go to tea with the Wyntons on the way back, they'd be delighted to see you, and I really think that you do want taking out of yourself."

"I was taken out of myself some time ago," replied Miss Lefain. "I really was, and I couldn't leave my things—though," she added with pathetic gratitude, "it is very, very kind of you."

"Your things would be quite safe, I'm sure," said Martha Pym, humouring her. "Who ever would come up here, this hour of a winter's day?"

"They do, oh, they do! And she might come back, prying and nosing and saying that it was all hers, all my beautiful china, hers!"

Miss Lefain squealed in her agitation and rising up, ran round the wall fingering with flaccid yellow hands the brilliant glossy pieces on the shelves.

"Well, then, I'm afraid that I must go, they'll be expecting me, and it's quite a long ride; perhaps some other time you'll come and see us?

"Oh, must you go?" quavered Miss Lefain dolefully. "I do like a little company now and then and I trusted you from the first—the others, when they do come, are always after my things and I have to frighten them away!"

"Frighten them away!" replied Martha Pym. "However do you do that?"

"It doesn't seem difficult, people are so easily frightened, aren't they?"

Miss Pym suddenly remembered that "Hartleys" had the reputation of being haunted—perhaps the queer old thing played on that; the lonely house with the grave in the garden was dreary enough around which to create a legend.

"I suppose you've never seen a ghost?" she asked pleasantly. "I'd rather like to see one, you know."

"There is no one here but myself," said Miss Lefain.

"So you've never seen anything? I thought it must be all nonsense. Still, I do think it rather melancholy for you to live here all alone."

Miss Lefain sighed:

"Yes, it's very lonely. Do stay and talk to me a little longer." Her whistling voice dropped cunningly. "And I'll give you the Crown Derby plate!"

"Are you sure you've really got it?" Miss Pym asked.

"I'll show you."

Fat and waddling as she was, she seemed to move very lightly as she slipped in front of Miss Pym and conducted her from the room, going slowly up the stairs—such a gross, odd figure in that clumsy dress with the fringe of white hair hanging on to her shoulders.

The upstairs of the house was as neat as the parlour, everything well in its place; but there was no sign of occupancy; the beds were covered with dust sheets, there were no lamps or fires set ready. "I suppose," said Miss Pym to herself, "she doesn't care to show me where she really lives."

But as they passed from one room to another, she could not help saying:

"Where do you live, Miss Lefain?"

"Mostly in the garden," said the other.

Miss Pym thought of those horrible health huts that some people indulged in.

"Well, sooner you than I," she replied cheerfully.

In the most distant room of all, a dark, tiny closet, Miss Lefain opened a deep cupboard and brought out a Crown Derby plate which her guest received with a spasm of joy, for it was actually that missing from her cherished set.

"It's very good of you," she said in delight. "Won't you take something for it, or let me do something for you?"

"You might come and see me again," replied Miss Lefain wistfully.

"Oh, yes, of course I should like to come and see you again."

But now that she had got what she had really come for, the plate, Martha Pym wanted to be gone; it was really very dismal and depressing in the house and she began to notice a fearful smell—the place had been shut up too long, there was something damp rotting somewhere, in this horrid little dark closet no doubt.

"I really must be going," she said hurriedly.

Miss Lefain turned as if to cling to her, but Martha Pym moved quickly away.

"Dear me," wailed the old lady. "Why are you in such haste?"

"There's—a smell," murmured Miss Pym rather faintly.

She found herself hastening down the stairs, with Miss Lefain complaining behind her.

"How peculiar people are—she used to talk of a smell."

"Well, you must notice it yourself."

Miss Pym was in the hall; the old woman had not followed her, but stood in the semi-darkness at the head of the stairs, a pale, shapeless figure.

Martha Pym hated to be rude and ungrateful but she could not stay another moment; she hurried away and

was in her cart in a moment—really—
that smell

"Good-bye!" she called out with false
cheerfulness, "and thank you so much!"

There was no answer from the house.

Miss Pym drove on; she was rather upset
and took another way than that by which she
had come, a way that led past a little house
raised above the marsh; she was glad to think
that the poor old creature at "Hartleys" had
such near neighbours, and she reined up the
horse, dubious as to whether she should call
someone and tell them that poor old Miss
Lefain really wanted a little looking after,
alone in a house like that, and plainly not
quite right in her head.

A young woman, attracted by the
sound of the governess cart, came to the
door of the house and, seeing Miss Pym,
called out, asking if she wanted the keys
of the house?

"What house?" asked Miss Pym.

"'Hartleys,' mum, they don't put a board out, as no one is likely to pass, but it's to be sold. Miss Lefain wants to sell or let it"

"I've just been up to see her."

"Oh, no, mum—she's been away a year, abroad somewhere, couldn't stand the place, it's been empty since then, I just run in every day and keep things tidy."

Loquacious and curious, the young woman had come to the fence; Miss Pym had stopped her horse.

"Miss Lefain is there now," she said. "She must have just come back."

"She wasn't there this morning, Mum, 'tisn't likely she'd come, either—fair scared she was, Mum, fair chased away, didn't dare move her china. Can't say I've noticed anything myself, but I never stay long— and there's a smell."

"Yes," murmured Martha Pym faintly, "there's a smell. What—what—chased her away?"

The young woman, even in that lonely place, lowered her voice.

"Well, as you aren't thinking of taking the place, she got an idea in her head that old Sir James—well, he couldn't bear to leave 'Hartleys,' Mum, he's buried in the garden, and she thought he was after her, chasing round them bits of china."

"Oh!" cried Miss Pym.

"Some of it used to be his, she found a lot stuffed away, he said they were to be left in 'Hartleys,' but Miss Lefain would have the things sold, I believe—that's years ago."

"Yes, yes," said Miss Pym with a sick look. "You don't know what he was like, do you?"

"No, Mum—but I've heard tell he was very stout and very old—I wonder who it was you saw up at 'Hartleys'?"

Miss Pym took a Crown Derby plate from her bag.

"You might take that back when you go," she whispered. "I shan't want it after all."

Before the astonished young woman could answer, Miss Pym had darted off across the marsh; that short hair, that earth-stained robe, the white socks, "I generally live in the garden."

Miss Pym drove away, breakneck speed, frantically resolving to mention to no one that she had paid a visit to "Hartleys," nor lightly again to bring up the subject of ghosts.

She shook and shuddered in the damp, trying to get out of her clothes and her nostrils—that indescribable smell.

arjorie Bowen (1885–1952) was a prolific British author who wrote historical romances, supernatural horror stories, popular history, and biographies.

eth is the cartoonist behind the comic-book series *Palookaville*, which started in the stone age as a pamphlet and is now a semi-annual hardcover. His comics have appeared in the *New York Times Magazine*, *Best American Comics*, and *McSweeney's Quarterly*. His illustrations have appeared in numerous publications including the cover of the *New Yorker*, the *Walrus*, and *Canadian Notes & Queries*. He is the subject of a recent documentary from the National Film board of Canada, *Seth's Dominion*.

Seth lives in Guelph, Ontario, with his wife Tania and their two cats in an old house he has named "Inkwell's End."

Publisher's Note: 'The Crown Derby Plate' was first published in 1931 in *Grace Latouche and the Warringtons*.

Library and Archives Canada Cataloguing in Publication

Bowen, Marjorie, 1885-1952, author
The Crown Derby plate : a ghost story for Christmas
/ Marjorie Bowen ; designed & decorated by Seth

Issued in print and electronic formats.
ISBN 978-1-77196-123-3 (paperback)
--ISBN 978-1-77196-124-0 (ebook)

I. Seth, 1962-, illustrator II. Title.

PR6003.O676C76 2016   823'.912   C2016-904584-6
                                    C2016-904585-4

Readied for the press by Daniel Wells
Illustrated and Designed by Seth
Copy-edited by Emily Donaldson
Typeset by Chris Andrechek

PRINTED AND BOUND IN CHINA